What happens when dinosaurs go to school? They spend a day full of reading, writing, arithmetic—and fun! They mix up squishy finger paints, and they swim in the pool. They practice playing tuba, and they learn how flowers grow. They munch on prickly pizza, brave the dino-slide and look forward to another day of school! Linda Martin's lyrical, rhyming text and comically detailed images show just how dino-mite school can be.

"Whether they're heading off to preschool or kindergarten, anxious children will be reassured and comforted by this jovial crew." —*Kirkus Reviews*

"There's a whole subgenre of rather earnest books intended to ease a child's way into school. Few, however, capture the fun quite so deftly as this dino romp."—*FamilyFun*

"Martin's lively illustrations in watercolor, acrylic, and pen and ink give children plenty to look at."—*Booklist*

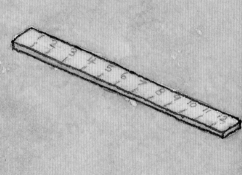

To Mom, Dad, Greg, Sue, and my Six Siblings

First paperback edition published in 2002 by Chronicle Books LLC.

Book design by Jane Coats.
Typeset in Stempel Garamond.
The illustrations in this book were rendered in watercolors, acrylic
and pen and ink.
Manufactured in China.

Library of Congress Cataloging-in-Publication Data
Martin, Linda, 1961-
When dinosaurs go to school / by Linda Martin. p. cm.
Summary: Dinosaurs spend a day at school with reading, writing,
arithmetic, music, finger paints, exercise, and pizza.
ISBN 0-8118-3514-6
[1. Dinosaurs-Fiction. 2. Schools-Fiction. 3. Stories in
rhyme.]   I. Title.
PZ8.3.M41216 Wf 2002
[E]--dc21
2001006475

Distributed in Canada by Raincoast Books
9050 Shaughnessy Street, Vancouver, British Columbia V6P 6E5

10 9 8 7 6 5 4 3 2 1

Chronicle Books LLC
85 Second Street, San Francisco, California 94105

www.chroniclekids.com

When Dinosaurs Go to School

Linda Martin

chronicle books · san francisco

When dinosaurs go off to school,
they like to look their best.
They wash behind their ears and scales,
and they're always nicely dressed.

They have a healthy breakfast
and eat a piece of fruit.
They give their Mom and Dad a hug,
and out the door they scoot.

Here comes the yellow school bus.
They find a seat inside.
They laugh and talk
and make new friends.
It's a very happy ride.

At last they reach the schoolhouse,
where some have come by car.

And some have even walked to school,
for they don't live very far.

The school bell rings to start the day.
How bright the classroom looks!
They start with spelling lessons,
then read their storybooks.

Next they paint with finger paints.
They're squishy, wet, and runny.
Some pictures turn out pretty nice,
and some look pretty funny.

Soon it's time to exercise.
So they head out for the gym,
where some learn how to kick a ball,
and others learn to swim.

When dinosaurs get hungry,
it must be time for lunch.
Today it's prickly pizza,
their favorite thing to munch!

The recess bell begins to ring.
It's time to play outside.
They all take turns at hopscotch
and ride the dino-slide.

Then come music lessons.
They learn a brand new song.

The music teacher swings a stick,
and taps his foot along.

Next, they learn their numbers,
and they learn how flowers grow.
But now the school day's over,
and it's time for them to go.

Dinosaurs all say goodbye,
and soon they're on their way.
But they'll be back tomorrow,
for another fun-filled day!

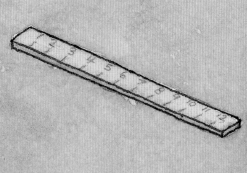

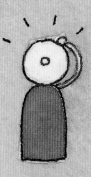

Linda Martin lives with her son, Alex, and pet iguana, Iggy, in beautiful Colorado Springs, Colorado. Her first book, *When Dinosaurs Go Visiting*, was published by Chronicle Books.

Praise for *When Dinosaurs Go Visiting:*
"The affable dinos in this adorable rhyming story have perfect manners."—*People*